The Greatest Fucking Moment in Sports

Other Books by Kevin L. Donihe

SHALL WE GATHER AT THE GARDEN?

OCEAN OF LARD (w/ Carlton Mellick III)

GRAPE CITY

HOUSE OF HOUSES

(*FORTHCOMING*):

VOLUPTUOUS SUNRISE

BUGABOO

THE FLAPPY PARTS

THE BONVILLE BONES

and others

The
Greatest Fucking
Moment in Sports

Kevin L. Donihe

ERASERHEAD PRESS
Portland, OR

ERASERHEAD PRESS
205 NE BRYANT
PORTLAND, OR 97211

WWW.ERASERHEADPRESS.COM

ISBN-10: 1-933929-52-9

ISBN-13: 978-1933929521

Author's Note:

I came up with this idea while watching the 2005 Tour de France on a TV that was not my own, though I did have permission to watch it.

Wait...

Come to think of it, I didn't have permission at all. (And I'm still in that house!)

      – Kevin L. Donihe
      April 23, 2006

Who is Oscar Legbo?:

Renowned Insectarian, role model, and now 7-time winner of the *Tour de Saucisse-Dommages*, Oscar Legbo is the reigning king of the sport of competitive bicycle racing; his popularity stretches across most, if not all, demographic lines. It is even rumored that a particular terrorist admires Oscar Legbo and has posters of him plastered upon the walls of his cave.

Something to Know About Legbo:

As a child, Oscar enjoyed killing bugs in borderline psychotic ways. If ever there was a Hitler-figure amongst the bug kingdom, it was surely Mr. Legbo. He filled bb guns with ball bugs (otherwise known as "rolly pollies") and shot them into snails. He also peeled bagworms from their cocoons and held their lower bodies with leaves intended to mimic bathtubs. Often, he would construct off-the-cuff monologues and pretend the bagworms were saying these things, usually before getting a thorn rammed through their heads as though they'd been murdered by a jilted lover, like some character out of a mystery novel, or by an assailant, like the unfortunate Frenchman from the painting.

If a bagworm survived long enough, he put a dramatic death soliloquy into its mouth.

In his early teens, after he built up the courage to experiment with gasoline, Oscar realized that a sardine can full of gas wouldn't explode when lit, and so he drew terminal baths, usually for snails, as their protective slime evaporated gradually and, for a short time, offered a buffer from the flames.

Eventually, Oscar grew to hate himself for the things

he'd done, especially after digging a series of grave-pits in which he left fuzzy caterpillars to rot, covering the hole with a twig roof and mud so they smothered and baked rather than being crushed by dirt, and some survived for weeks before finally turning into thick and smelly goop.

One night, after stirring a particularly deep and noxious pit, he felt caterpillar souls scrape at him as he tried to sleep, wiggling beneath his covers and begging for surcease. The next morning, when he contemplated the food he ate, he imagined heat-softened corpses were layered inside it and, when he stirred his potatoes, a familiar decomposition smell arose from them.

Oscar threw his food away and vomited, off and on, for almost an hour.

In the end, it had been fuzzy caterpillars that inaugurated his transformation, but they were no different from the bagworms, the slugs, the rolly pollies, and other insects he'd murdered. To kill any bug, he realized, was unacceptable, if not a crime.

It was after reaching this epiphany at age 19 that he devoted his life to the sport of competitive bicycle racing. At first, it was a simple diversion that kept him from doing what he sometimes still wanted to do, but, with the constant aid and support of Coach Fernardo de Papa, racing supplanted killing bugs as the crux of his day-to-day existence.

To this day, Oscar wears a uniform that features a five-pointed star, and upon each point sits a different bug: a camel cricket, a caterpillar, a bagworm, a katydid, and a June bug. Below them, a lone snail coils around a sprig of ivy. He also wears a pair of floppy antennae while racing, and last year added a dark spot on his uniform right above his heart.

It, of course, signifies a bb pellet wound.

LADYBUG

a poem by Oscar Legbo

Ladybug, ladybug
- with me is where you belong.

Ladybug, ladybug
- be it Eros or be it Agape

how could our love
ever be wrong?

Preparation for the 89th Annual *Tour de Saucisse-Dommages*:

Oscar pedaled with not one, but two cinderblocks strapped beneath his feet. His hands were wrapped in barbed wire and, just for added effect, handcuffed to the handlebar. He wore nothing but an antique loincloth that Coach de Papa had personally chosen for him.

The coach had outfits, too—a series of costumes that accompanied seven alternating dioramas that were hoisted atop a high school homecoming float, which was then tied to the rear of Legbo's bike.

Coach de Papa was known for his unusual training techniques. Some days, he was a chariot racer, and Oscar his mechanical, wheel-legged horse. Other days, he was Satan himself, and Oscar just another lost soul forced to serve a master. Today, however, he was King Neptune, replete with trident and flowing seafoam green cape, though he still wore the same little red running shorts that he'd worn, non-stop, for the last twenty years. He also braided his beard for the occasion and wove a small starfish into its center. Life-sized plastic dolphins, positioned to look as though they were leaping from the sea, bracketed Coach de Papa.

Oscar was likewise a dolphin—a sleek, aquatic slave —and would remain so for eight-to-twelve more hours. Sometimes Coach de Papa demanded that he create dolphin noises, and, if they sounded phony, would lash him with his ever-present whip.

Legbo International paid for the costumes, the dioramas, and the float. The company didn't mind because Coach de Papa's excesses inspired results.

"I am Neptune!" he roared. "How dare you not give me 100%!" Coach de Papa cracked his whip against Oscar's naked back. "*Faster*! You're a dolphin, not a manatee for Christ's sake!"

"Yes, Coach de Papa! I am a dolphin!"

"Not Coach de Papa! *King Neptune*!"

"Yes, Neptune!"

Coach de Papa threw a conch shell at his head. "*King*! King Neptune!"

"Yes, *King*! *King Neptune*!"

He cracked the whip again. "You only need to say 'king' once!"

Oscar trudged on. Fifteen miles had passed, but thirty-five more loomed ahead. He hung his head briefly, an attempt to center and relax himself. Bringing his gaze down to the road, he saw a bug—a large, black beetle with pinchers—less than a foot away, crawling into the path of his bike.

He turned the handlebar sharply, sparing the bug. Oscar let out a sigh, but then heard a loud *creak* behind him. He turned to see the float, tilted at a 45-degree angle and keeling fast. Atop it, Coach de Papa struggled to maintain his balance.

It pained Oscar to see such a great man stumble; he straightened the path of his bike, but the float continued to lean,

Coach de Papa clutching the Styrofoam representation of a mermaid until it broke in two. Then he tumbled out onto the road, and the float fell atop him.

Oscar jumped off the bike and slid out of the cinderblock shoes. Still, he dragged the bicycle behind him. Coach de Papa had the only keys to the handcuffs.

He ran to the overturned float but couldn't make himself look to the side of it. Coach de Papa had never fallen before; Oscar didn't know the man could fall. Finally, he looked, and, at that moment, had to make himself breathe.

Coach de Papa's legs were pinned by the float and his trident—which was real and not a prop—had impaled him straight through the chest.

Oscar leaned over his body. "Coach de Papa?"

"Oscar." He coughed up a blood-gout.

"Don't talk." Oscar tilted Coach de Papa's back in an effort to remove the trident.

He scowled. "Please don't do that."

"Quiet, Coach. If you just let me—"

"*Don't touch the goddamn trident! When you wiggle it, it hurts like a fucker!*"

"Please, Coach, let me do *something*!"

"Oscar," he said, his voice now a groan, another blood-bubble in his mouth. "Just—just tell me one thing, okay?"

"Anything!"

"Why did you do this?"

"I—I did it for the bug, Coach. It would have been crushed!"

Coach de Papa gritted his teeth. "What the fuck, Oscar."

"I didn't know this would happen! I never meant to

hurt you. I—I love you, Coach de Papa!" Then Oscar had to turn away; he couldn't stand the way his coach stared at him.

"I mean, really. What the—"

And then he was gone.

The Press Room, Just Before the Race:

Oscar was attired in bright, skin-tight racing gear, his hair slicked back and his teeth finely scrubbed with tiny loofah brushes just minutes before by a team of handlers. His body was lean and taut, and reporters—male and female—oogled his physique for longer than necessary, amazed to find no indications that the Ebola virus had traveled through his system the summer beforehand. He had been the first to survive the disease, encountered on a wild safari tour with two young American men, both of whom had pledged to a fraternity. They died horrible, painful deaths, and it appeared as though Legbo would as well—until he didn't. Medical professionals viewed his recovery as miraculous, but Oscar neither confirmed nor denied the supernatural. His reply: "What happens, happens."

He took to the stage, and members of the press corps fell onto each other, a mound of writhing humanity.

"Oscar! Oscar!" one shouted. "How do you feel about racing so soon after the death of your long-time coach, Fernardo de Papa?"

Oscar spent a moment in thought. "I loved my coach —loved him like no other man—and his loss hangs heavy on me, but he would have been very disappointed had I failed to race today."

"And is it true that you caused his death?"

"It was an accident, a horrible, horrible accident." He exhaled slowly. "But, in the end, Coach de Papa died so that another might live."

"By 'another' do you mean a bug?"

"Yes. Specifically, I mean a big black beetle."

An elderly reporter stood: "What's your opinion of the German rider, Helmut Starb?"

Oscar's bottom lip twitched. "I'd rather not talk about Helmet, thank you very much."

"But he's your strongest competitor; some commentators have predicted his victory."

Now his left eye twitched. "Yes. Yes, I know this."

"Surely, you want to say *something* about such a bright and rising young—"

"*I said I'd rather not talk about him*! Next question, please!"

That reporter sat and another stood: "If you win today, whom will you do it for? God? Country? Family? Coach de Papa?"

He did not hesitate. "I do this not for God, or country, or family, or even Coach de Papa, though I love him more than the last three combined." He slammed his fist against the podium. "No! I do it for bugs!"

His passion shot across the room and made all the journalists in attendance buckle, hitch, and waver in their seats, or fall from them and do what Oscar now thought of as *the electric salmon* across the floor. He didn't know why this happened at every press conference since his return

16

from Africa. It had concerned him at first, but he didn't mind now. He found their display weird but touching, and it stroked his ego.

One, an Asian reporter, finally recovered enough to speak, though she remained in a supine position:

"Do you realize, Mr. Legbo, that most Americans willfully and without remorse kill as many bugs as possible on a given day, and that there's a certain fetish that involves the stomping of insects by nubile women for voyeuristic, sexual pleasure?"

"Yes, I am aware of these things, and it irks me to no end. People can have whatever quirks and kinks they want, but leave the fucking bugs out of it!"

Intersplice:
The Office of Standards and Practices:

"He didn't just fucking say *fucking*, did he?"

The man nodded.

"Run the eight-second delay!"

"Already on it."

Press (*cont.*):

The press lady cowered in the corner, her hands over her face. Oscar looked down, recognized her fear, and, in an instant, came back to himself.

"Oh, sorry."

The woman did not—could not—respond.

"When I get worked up about bugs, I sometimes black out." Oscar smoothed creases in his racing uniform and returned to the podium. "I don't imagine it'll happen again, at least not today."

He continued his answer as reporters dusted off their clothes and rose slowly from the floor:

"But yes, I am aware of our society's indifference to bugs. And maybe it's right. Maybe a bug's death doesn't matter, not in the long run, but this is my personal battle, so let me wage it in the way I see fit."

Another reporter: "And what was it that made you believe the way you do? Was it some grand epiphany, and, if so, what was the nature of this epiphany?"

"You know my story; I've never been less than honest with you. I used to be an evil, evil man who did evil, evil things to bugs, but I don't want to say any more than that because I know children—millions and millions of them—are watching right now."

"Do you ever think you're being too hard on yourself?"

"No. This burden is mine to carry, so I carry it." Oscar drew in a deep breath, held it in for a few seconds, and exhaled slowly. "But it is a sweet, sweet burden, indeed."

"And why is it sweet?"

"Without it, I would have committed suicide long ago. My guilt was strong, but my love and my sense of duty were stronger, and they brought me back. Once this happened, I realized that love and a sense of duty can bring *anyone* and *anything* back, if both are pursued with the right heart."

"And that's why we love you!" screamed a man on

fire in the back row. Yet another fan—doused head-to-toe in gasoline—had slipped into a press conference with the desire to self-immolate.

Oscar left the podium. He didn't even realize he had done so until he was standing by the man, his hand atop a flaming shoulder.

"Self-immolation is not recommended, sir."

At that moment, the fire receded. The man looked at his hands and slid them down his face. There was no charred or bloody skin.

"Wait," he said. "Shouldn't I be dead?"

"Probably, but why are you fussing when you're not?"

The man did not reply, at least not audibly. He nodded his head back and forth, too lost in Legbo's eyes to notice the angry-looking men who stalked up behind him.

* * * *

Once the fan had been escorted away by armed security, the barrage of questions surged anew.

One: "How did you touch him?"

Another: "Are your hands coated in fire retardant?"

A third: "Are you the Second Coming?"

Oscar shook his head. "Sometimes I don't know what I'm going to do until I do it or what's going to happen until it happens. It's the power of agape love working through me, and, hopefully, it shall soon work through you, too."

A reporter piped up from the second row: "And how will that be done?"

"This win—this monumental and historic win—will

return the love that's now missing on this planet. These words may sound like candy and rainbows to you, but such is the intended nature of my working." He took a hearty chug from a water glass.

"And how do you know that this—uh—*working* will work?"

Oscar smiled winsomely. "Because you love me, and because I love you."

Parts of the room erupted in applause. Two or three more people went up in flames.

"Now, if you'll excuse me, I must prepare for the race."

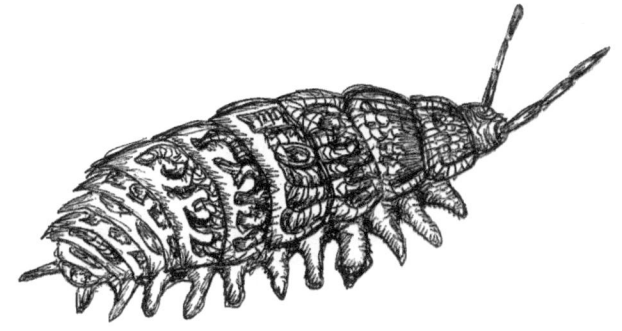

ROLLY POLLIE
a poem by Oscar Legbo

Shrink me to the size of a pin.
Let me ride you -
my sleek, black friend
- into an underground fantasyland
where you'll encase me in your shell
and roll me up in beauty.

Legbo's Pre-Race Ritual:

Oscar dressed for the press conference, but couldn't perform his pre-race ritual with clothes on, so he lost them.

First, he touched the plushy, stuffed ladybug that crouched on his dresser. He'd named it Charley. On the road, he slept with it. At home, it had a permanent place on his sofa, joining him each night to watch TV after a long day of practice. Oscar's eyes rolled back into his head as he made contact with the thing, feeling as though an electric pulse had been transmitted through the stuffed bug and into him.

His synapses now prepared for the experience, he contorted himself into the lotus position and, with his index finger, touched his nasal chakra. An old Hindu had told him that nasal charkas didn't exist, but that man was a fool. How could they not exist when he was touching his own and feeling it radiate through all the subtle pathways of his body?

When the time was right, Oscar recited his customary incantation: *"June Bug! June Bug! Skitterbug! Ra! Atman! Ra!"*

At that moment, all the bug souls he had ever freed from Earthly bodies enveloped him, stretching outward from his core in a massive spiral. They stared at him without approval and without dismay. Then they began to spin, emitting colors and lights until, with a sound like a vacuum, they were sucked into his body where the memory of their Earthly pain and hate could fuel him for the race.

When the ritual was over, Oscar relaxed in a corpse-pose until he'd be late at the starting line if he didn't get up and get dressed.

He slipped back into his racing uniform and placed the floppy antennae—an item he only wore when racing, as it functioned as a special receptor—on his head. Oscar then looked into the mirror and gave himself a grin. It was now time, time to go out and show the world what it meant to love.

KATYDID
a poem by Oscar Legbo

You're all bug,
though you look part plant.

You feed on leaves and stems,
flowers and fruits.

My flesh is now your leaf.
Suck my stem
and partake of my flowers and fruits
whenever you please.

At the Starting Line:

Oscar allowed his body to fuse with the bicycle as he awaited the starting gun. He imagined flesh becoming steel and steel becoming flesh until there was no real separation between the two.

He was returned to himself by the words of a Belgian bastard whose name was Decker *Something*. Oscar couldn't remember his last. Decker was red-haired, stockier than most riders and had a tattoo of a bicycle stretched across his face, with his eyes serving as the center of the wheels. "Nice antennae, Oscar," he said. "Know where I can get a pair?"

Oscar admired Decker's devotion to the sport, but was tired of his taunting, school-bully ways. "Oh, go to hell," he whispered under his breath.

Helmut Starb, future racing champion and friend of the Belgian, snickered. Oscar turned and scowled; he hated even looking at him. His nose was reminiscent of a bratwurst and his stringy hair of a pile of sauerkraut that hung out over a wrinkly brown skullcap. Oscar didn't know what purpose the skullcap served, or what it was supposed to signify, if anything.

"Hey, Oscar," he said. "Look at the bottom of my shoe!"

Then Helmut showed him his sole where a large grasshopper was smashed yet twitching. Oscar felt sympathetic pain, and then irrational, all-encompassing rage. He imagined ramming an oversized thorn into the man's head, shooting his unresponsive body into that of another bug killer via cannon, or dumping him down a personal death-pit, sealing it, and then stirring his muck after a few months had elapsed.

"You like this, no?" Helmut looked to his left. "Oh, a cricket, too!"

"Don't you—"

Helmut smashed the cricket, grinding it into the pavement with his heel for a few more seconds than necessary. When finished, he raked his shoe clean, leaving a black smear on the road.

Another rider—a too-thin Frenchman with a spiky unibrow who Oscar sometimes saw alongside Helmut and Decker—smirked, but said nothing. Oscar remembered neither his first nor his last name, and didn't care if he ever found them out.

"I can't believe it," Helmut said, and both the Belgian and the Frenchman turned at the sound of his voice. "An ant!"

Oscar couldn't take it anymore. "Bug killing motherfuckers!" he screamed to an international audience of millions, as there was no eight-second delay.

The Race Begins:

It had taken him a while to calm down, up until the moment the starting gun fired. Finally, his hands were able to become vices and his legs pumping pistons. Sometimes, he imagined his penis was likewise a piston, but that was too distracting to visualize during important races.

The terrain was so familiar that he could negotiate it with his eyes closed. Every bend and every curve were like the supple contours of the women he could never quite convince himself to touch. *The bitches—the evil, horrible bitches!* His mind screamed. *Oh God, I love them still!*

Oscar forced himself to snap out of it; he looked up at the sky. It was overcast, gray and threatening, and the air around him was chilly.

Perhaps the weather wouldn't change for the worse, but change seemed inevitable. Though he had raced in less than favorable conditions, those races hadn't been 48-hours removed from the death of his coach. Usually, he was able to toss distractions aside and get into—if not become—the race. Today, however, felt different and *wrong*.

Maybe that Helmut bastard really had what it took to

become champion. Maybe it was time for him to retire, anyway.

Maybe it was *past* time.

He made himself snap out of it again. *Oscar Legbo was a winner, is a winner, and shall be a winner*, he thought, and applied pressure to the radial axle bar.

Another Thing to Know About Legbo:

The part to which Legbo had applied pressure was not a 'radial axle bar'—bicycles don't have such a part.

During his early training, he called the axle a *dum-dum* and spokes *ree-dees*. He had equally nonsensical names for all the other parts, too. Oscar's immaturity drove Coach de Papa to the brink of madness, but he suffered through it, for he knew he had a racing prodigy on his hands.

As Oscar got older—in his late 20s—he started calling parts like the steering system 'radial axle bars,' thus trading in a few (but not all) of the baby sounds for names he imagined were more sophisticated and scientific-sounding. Still, he refused to call any of the parts by—or even learn—their actual names.

This is a tightly kept secret no one but Oscar and those closest to him—and, of course, the CEO of *Legbo International*—know.

The Race Continues:

Earlier, it had appeared as though the sky might crack open, but things had changed. The temperature had risen, becoming warm without being hot, and, for the last ten or so miles, there hadn't been a cloud in the sky.

Maybe these were good omens.

Oscar felt silly for having worried. Helmut didn't stand a chance, and Coach de Papa—God bless him—was surely smiling down upon this race, beaming with postmortem pride.

Perhaps, Oscar thought, *it was he who cleared the skies…*

Then he noticed something in the road in front of him.

At first, he thought it was a bunch of loose gravel; perhaps some had slid down from the opposing hill during the last rainstorm. Then he noticed that the things moved, skittering like...like...

Bugs.

Oscar ground his bike to a halt just in time. He looked out over the mess of writhing insect life before him—crickets and rolly pollies and katydids and June bugs and fireflies and praying mantises; there were far too many—in terms of both number and variety—to have gotten there on their own volition, and the fireflies and June bugs had all had their wings clipped.

He jumped off his bike and leaned it against an incline on the side of the road, scowling as he thought of Helmut, Decker the Belgian, and the Frenchman. He didn't suspect the other riders had anything to do with this, as they weren't assholes, at least not to his face.

"I'll save you, my babies!" he shouted, picking up a handful of bugs and placing them—facing away from the road—in the grass. "I won't let bad wheels crush you!"

But they kept returning, like the pavement had been sprinkled with pheromones.

"No!" he shrieked. "Don't go back there! Bad bugs! *Bad bugs*!"

Oscar heard the sound of approaching bicycles and looked up.

Helmut waved at him. "See you at the finish line, Oscar!" As he passed, he made sure to smash as many bugs as possible.

"Rot in Hell!" Oscar screamed, shaking his fist until he could not longer see Helmut.

Then Decker the Belgian and the smirking Frenchman passed him, followed, in time, by all the other riders in the 89th annual *Tour de Saucisse-Dommages*.

And Oscar wove in and out of traffic; saving as many insects as he could and screaming while others were crushed.

SNAIL

a poem by Oscar Legbo

In truth,
you're not a bug,
but that doesn't mean
you haven't left
an indelible slime trail
across my heart.

In the Channel 5 Newsroom:

Anchorlady Jane (*clutches a handful of papers from which she is clearly not reading*): For the first time in the history of his involvement with the *Tour de Saucisse-Dommages*, Oscar Legbo is dead last.

Anchorman Tim (*takes a quick gulp from a coffee cup emblazoned with Oscar Legbo's head*): This is a sad moment for America. Oscar, listen to your fans when we say, "lay off the bugs, just lay off them."

Anchorlady Jane: Everybody needs a mission, Tim. It's what makes life worth living.

Anchorman Tim (*flushes red*): Not if it costs him the race! Look, I respect and admire Oscar's dedication. Hell, I even quit stomping bugs for a year because of him!

Anchorlady Jane: Why don't we take a look at what went wrong?

(*Cut to pre-recorded video of Oscar dodging bikes and*

leaping to the ground, saving bugs or shrieking like a girl when they splatter at his feet.)

Anchorman Tim: See what I mean? That's just pathetic! (*He gets up and looks about the studio, first beneath the desk, then on the walls, then on the floor. Finally, after almost a minute, he arises with something in his hand.*) Hah! Found one.

Anchorlady Jane: Found what, Tim?

Anchorman Tim: A bug, Jane. (*He brings it over to the camera, so close now that his face fills its frame. Then he takes the bug and smashes its guts across the lens.*) See that, Oscar? See the first bug I've killed in a frickin' year? (*His gaze becomes distant.*) This is my sacrifice to you.

Anchorlady Jane: Now, Tim, we don't want to upset the members of our audience. You know many of them have adopted Oscar's non-violent stance toward bugs.

Anchorman Tim (*comes to himself*): Forget about them! And forget about the bugs, too! Get your head in the race, Oscar, before you lose it!

Helmut Starb:

Helmut had the strength and dedication to defeat Legbo; he knew this. The stars just hadn't aligned yet. But he was sick of waiting on them, so he paid his cousin 100 Euro to collect a bunch of bugs and dump them on the raceway.

Besides, it was time—*past* time— for Oscar to fall. Before, even he had liked Lebgo. Now, he saw him for what he was: just another glory hog. And to what end? *Bugs*? Helmut scoffed at insects. They were pansy; they were gay. The walri, however, were different.

Helmut was a proud walri-man.

He knew the plural of *walrus* was *walruses*, but he nevertheless thought and said *walri*. Though grammatically incorrect, he felt that the word better encapsulated their spirit. Walri were big and strong and had large brown phalluses and even larger ivory tusks. At times, he went out to his patio late at night and made sensual walri mating sounds; fuck a bunch of neighbors.

He wore the walri-skin skullcap to get in touch with the most admirable walri qualities: their toughness, their steadfastness, and, most of all, their ability to survive in harsh, arctic conditions. There was also something vaguely mystical about them, something that made it seem as though they knew something that humans did not. Helmut felt on the verge of groking this *something*, and it would only be a matter of time until the mysteries of the walri were revealed in full. He didn't feel their spirits surge through his skullcap, though; he wasn't a bona fide kook like Legbo.

When not riding bicycles, Helmut rode walri at the aquarium in his hometown, ostensibly for the amusement of children, but really for his own. At times, he considered sneaking in late at night to have carnal relations with one or more walri, but all the walri at the aquarium were male, and he was heterosexual.

The Belgian understood his singular passion, and so Helmut converted him, made him a *Walrite*. He'd given him a skullcap identical to his own and led him through an elaborate initiation ceremony involving a dagger and a golden chalice brimming with walri semen. He had accepted this offering, but Helmut was disappointed to see Decker not wearing the skullcap at the starting line; he had told him to put it on, but not before meditating for at least an hour beforehand.

The Frenchman was more stubborn than Decker; he refused to even partake from the cup or carve the image of *The Grand Tusk* into his chest. Helmut wasn't ready to let him back down, not yet anyway. He would just have to take things slowly with Pierre, just as he would have to take things slowly with the world once his popularity eclipsed that of Legbo, thus paving the way for the Age of Walri to begin.

On Mile 18 of the *Tour de Saucisse-Dommages*:

Oscar realized that the last bike had passed him. The bugs were in no further danger, but he was in danger of losing the race.

There was only one thing to do.

He got onto his bicycle and prepared to enter the Zen state, or what he liked to call the *nobody-can-touch-me-not-even-myself* state. It was a dimension he discovered, accidentally, during his third running of the *Tour de Saucisse-Dommages*. In it, time and space became meaningless, and, if he gave himself utterly to the moment, then that moment would carry him anywhere he needed to go.

He closed his eyes, blanked his mind, and imagined himself far away from the race, perhaps on some enchanted isle, dancing with human-sized rolly pollies amongst daffodils and lady slippers as bugs of various types and sizes looked on. Here, they no longer cared that they had been murdered, for this was a place far beyond caring.

Oscar continued to live in this world until he sensed the presence of another. He opened his eyes and saw that he now raced beside Helmut. Still, he did not exit the Zen state, just its accompanying world.

"Take a look at this, Oscar Bugbo!" Helmut shouted. "It's part of a collection I've had since I was eight!"

Oscar turned to him, but he did not scowl or shout. Such things were impossible in the Zen state. He just looked at and through Helmut, seeing him for the sick, sad, and desperate little man that he was. Oscar would have laughed, had laughter itself been possible.

Helmut reached into a fanny pack tied around his hips and brought out a handful of dry bugs, their bodies still skewered on pins. Then he threw them, most of the bugs either missing or rebounding from Oscar. Others, however, stuck to his racing suit.

Helmut laughed, thinking Oscar might shriek or flail his arms and lose control of the bike, but these poor, abused corpses served as fuel. In the Zen state, he was more receptive to their spirit energy, still clinging to long dead and dried husks. They radiated through him in hard, steady currents. Soon, Oscar perceived these currents as inseparable from his body. He then flew like an insect himself, through the wind, leaving the German clutching a handful of dead and now useless bugs.

In the Channel 5 Newsroom:

Anchorman Tim: This just in: there has been a dramatic change in lead position at the 89th Annual *Tour de Saucisse-Dommages*.

(*Cut to a playback of Oscar Legbo overtaking Helmut Starb, which is superimposed over the image of a flapping American flag.*)

Anchorlady Jane: It's amazing that Oscar Legbo can go from last to first place in such short time, but this man is no stranger to breaking the odds.

Anchorman Tim: My god! (*His eyes roll back into his head.*) Think how well endowed this guy must be!

Anchorlady Jane: Yes, Tim, he must truly have a python down there, but Helmut Starb—said to be Oscar's biggest competition—is still 100% in the race, as are Belgium's Decker Rasmussen and France's Pierre LaChaise.

Anchorman Tim (*says beneath his breath*): Damn foreigners.

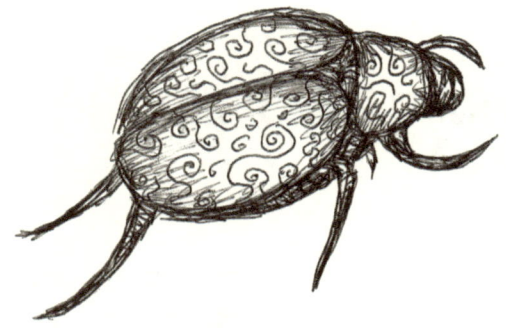

JUNE BUG

a poem by Oscar Legbo

Break the string
that tethers you
to hateful fingers.

Fly free!
Revolution now!

Reclaim spirit;
let would-be captors
sulk on the ground.

In Dreams:

Augmented by swirling bug spirits, the dream world now enveloped him fully. Whether Helmut was still throwing his bug collection at him, Oscar didn't know, and didn't care.

In this world, the rolly pollie suddenly paused its exotic, Eastern-flavored dance and pressed itself firmly against Oscar's torso. Its seemingly hundreds of tiny, almost threadlike legs pulled down his zipper.

It was time for the happy ending.

But, Oscar realized, there would be no time for the usual coda. Zen-ing out was perfect when a quick burst was needed, but not when his physical attributes and conditioning were enough to see him through. He sensed this was now the case, and it was unwise to take advantage of so precious a blessing.

He broke the embrace. "I'm sorry baby, but this'll have to wait. I've got a Tour to win."

The rolly pollie looked sad, but Oscar knew that it understood.

He turned to face his audience: "Bye fireflies," he said.

"Bye."

"Bye June Bugs, katydids, and cicadas!"

They said the same thing as the fireflies.

After everyone had said their goodbyes, the insects and the world they inhabited began to waver. When the scene faded, it did not do so into black, but into a backdrop of squiggly, multi-colored fractals. Once they were gone, Oscar would be back in his old world.

The last fractal fizzled out thirty seconds later, and a black blur leapt into the road in front of him.

Helmut Starb:

Helmut saw the black blob, too, but saw it for what it was: a man in a ninja suit who jumped from dense shrubbery lining the road and chopped off Oscar Legbo's head.

Helmut almost fell from his bike, thinking that, perhaps, the ninja would go after him next. Though over 50 feet away, he was the closest rider to Legbo.

But the assailant didn't as much as look at him, and disappeared quickly into the shrubs.

Helmut also bore witness to the aftermath. Oscar remained astride his bike, his neck shooting a fountain of red high into the air. It was vile, disgusting, and Helmet felt sick right down to his core. He wanted to vomit, but knew that he couldn't—everything would become slippery and he would wreck—so he held it in.

As he waited for his gorge to settle, Helmut came to a certain realization. He smiled at that moment, though he still wanted to throw up.

In the Channel 5 Newsroom:

Anchorlady Jane: What you are seeing is real.

(Cut from the anchor to the replay of Oscar Legbo's decapitation. A man in a ninja suit jumps into the road and strikes at Lebgo with a sword. His head flies off his shoulders and hits a small Ukrainian boy in the crowd. Though the boy is fazed but unhurt, his mother invokes a curse from her tribal god, but no one hears it. Pandemonium erupts as a blood geyser shoots from Oscar Legbo's neck stump, the flow of it so strong and red that it would be beautiful overlaid against the afternoon sky had it not come from a person.)

Anchorlady Jane (voice-over): Oscar Legbo, America's golden boy of professional bicycle racing, is dead.

(The decapitation replay ends—after looping over six times, three of those six times in slow motion; cut back to the studio.)

Anchorman Tim: Oh my fucking god, Jane! That blood geyser

was pumping from his neck like crazy! It didn't look like it would ever end!

Anchorlady Jane: I don't think you're supposed to take our Lord's name in vain or say 'fucking,' on the airwaves, Tim. (*Eyes widen.*) Oh fuck, now I said it!

(*A voice off-stage, perhaps that of a stagehand who has just fallen from a ladder or plugged something into a wall socket while standing in a puddle*: "Fuck!")

Anchorman Tim: This is worse than the time North Korea dumped loads of nuclear waste off the San Franciscan coast and laughed and screamed taunting, homophobic insults to those who lived in the vicinity.

Anchorlady Jane: I don't remember that happening, Tim.

Anchorman Tim: The only thing you ever remember is who you had to blow to get this job! (*He composes himself.*) Sorry about that, folks. I'm a diehard Oscar Legbo fan, so this is a very trying time. At any rate, I have been informed that the President is making a statement. We will now go live to that.

(*Cut to the President. He sits in a chair in the oval office, looking slightly disheveled, like someone has awoken him from a nap.*)

President: Today, the sports world—and America as a whole —experienced a tragedy beyond compare. No words I say will console you; I understand this. (*The president leans in closer to the camera.*) But please—I beg of you—do not allow this one act of cowardice to serve as a catalyst for American-on-Ninja violence. I speak from experience when I say that most ninjas are good, caring people who do what they do out of an overarching sense of loyalty, honor, and decency. Again, please do not riot against or in any way harm these treasured members of our national community. Thank you for listening, America; my heart travels out to you today.

(*Cut back to the news desk at Channel Five.*)

Anchorlady Jane: I didn't realize we had ninjas in our community. But, if we do, I stand by our President in saying please—citizens of America—do not harm them or torch their residences or businesses. What we need now is *healing*, not more pain.

Anchorman Tim: I say let them burn.

(*An assistant—who is also a Legbo fan and, in fact, wears a Legbo shirt—rushes into camera range. He whispers into the anchorman's ear; Tim's eyes widen.*)

Anchorman Tim (*to assistant*): What? He's still going? Oh my God...

Ninja:

Before his head can strike the pavement, I'm in surrounding woods, away from the gaze and energy of the crowd, though I still hear the sounds of chaos—screams and shouts and sirens. I hate such noises, but they are constant companions in my line of work.

I am a ninja, my body sleek and well oiled. Though I function as a killing machine, I do not despise my prey; I respect and honor them. Once dispatched, their blood becomes my own and, as it flows through my veins, strangers become brothers.

My target was Oscar Legbo. I had to track him and slaughter him like a beast of burden. Perhaps, in a different life, I might have met this man over a bowl of miso soup (brown not red) where we'd chat for a while, and, if we were both into it, smoke *heycheeba*, the ninja equivalent of herb. That was not to be. Rather, my sword separated his head swiftly and painlessly from his body. Such is the blessing— and the power and precision—of my blade.

But something uncharacteristic happened today. Right before I struck, things went fuzzy all the sudden. The ground felt like rubber beneath my feet and there was this little buzzer that went off in my head, and it just wouldn't quit. It was like I had a computer up there, something electrical that churned away and made me think things that I didn't want thought.

"*Do it!*" an angry voice screamed inside my skull. "*Do it now!*"

I refused—a ninja does things when *he* wants—but then what felt like angry, long-nailed hands took hold of me, first via my brain, then via my nut sack.

"Okay, okay!" I head-screamed. "I'll do it now!"

The buzzing faded as I lept from the crowd and into the roadway. Then I let my sword grow wings and fly.

* * * *

I walk through the woods until I can no longer hear the sounds of chaos; I find myself at a stream. It looks inviting, so I sit at its bank, drinking water and contemplating what I've done.

It is a singularly pleasant environment, but I wish I could sit by Legbo instead. It's only the density of the crowd that makes this impossible. Even in his present condition, we could converse, as I'm sure his head still lives. Such is the magic of my blade.

Once, I sat and talked with a noble farmer for over an hour after his decapitation. We became friends, and I told him about my life and he told me about his. In the end, I hated to see the fire go out of his eyes and hated even more the fact that it was my sword that had snuffed it, but such is the way of things.

With lingering heartache, I trace in my mind the events that brought me here today. I realize, with some confusion, that

I don't even know who had ordered me to assassinate Oscar Legbo. I just remember being led into a room and forced into a chair, a big sturdy one with a carved wolf's head on the top. Another man was there, too, my nameless and faceless benefactor. He leaned into me, his countenance still lost in shadow, and said: "Do you or don't you?"

"I do," was my response. I remember this clearly now, though I don't think I was wearing the same clothes or —and this may sound weird—the same face when I said it.

No matter. There's really nothing to gain in thinking about the past, but I do it anyway. Though ninja, I am also human, so I get sentimental at times, or sad. But I never get lost in these emotions; I just suck it up and do what I have to do, and now my spirit and the spirit of Oscar Legbo have bonded. We are one, and I will honor his constant presence as it trails me through this life of shadows.

Inside Oscar's severed head:

I am severed; I am severed and I am dead. I am a deadhead. Leghead dead. Bohead Leg.

Wait. That's not right. That's not what (who?) I am. Not at all. I am Osdead BoLego. Or is it Deadleg Bo or, perhaps, just Leghead?

No, none of those seem right. I am... I am... I am... *Oscar Legbo.* Yes. I am Oscar Legbo—bicycle racer extraordinaire and friend to bugs everywhere—and someone has just decapitated me, ruining both my race and my working. It's odd that I'm worrying about such things when I'm dead. You'd think I might have something else on my mind, namely *nothing.*

But, nevertheless, *something* is on my mind. I'm not entirely sure that it's possible, but, if I can get back in control of myself, I might just be able to finish this race, and maybe even the working, too; I have to focus on the here and now, and make myself win. It doesn't matter how many tours I've completed in the past; if I can't finish this one, then I'm a failure. My body is superb and conditioned, and it knows every twist, turn, and bend of this course, but it can't go on forever without a guide.

PRAYING MANTIS
a poem by Oscar Legbo

Don't use your pinching legs
against me.

Don't bite off my head
if and when we mate.

Just pray for me.

Give me the strength I need
to race through this world
and never go astray.

At the moment, I see only the landscape in front of me tilted at an extreme angle, but maybe, if I put all my energy into it, I can reach out to and control my body. A kindly old monk taught me how to do this with other bodies once, during one of my travels to Tibet. It was difficult at first; I just stared for hours at the darkness behind my eyelids as my instructor chanted indecipherable words in the background—but, finally, I was able to see, and able to hone in on what I saw, so much so that I was able to spy upon Coach de Papa bathing at home, thousands of miles away. As he sat there, unaware of my scrutiny, I made his hands wash his lower body, slowly and with small circular motions that he seemed to enjoy. He was very clean by the time I finished with him.

No. I'm getting lost in the past. I must pull away from it because it's far too distracting, and there's no time for distractions.

My eyes close. In darkness, I am able to hone my concentration, and I concentrate so hard that veins would have probably burst had blood flowed through them still. Once I feel ready, I grab hold of my essence and project it in eddies so as to locate the rest of me.

Yes! Yes, I think I've found it! But no, it's just another racer, the Belgian bastard with bugs on his shoes. I shiver upon realization and break the connection quickly. Finally, I feel myself: the unique presence of a moving body without a head.

I latch onto myself just in time. If I'd stayed in the dead zone (or was it the zone-before-the-dead-zone?) any longer my body would have lost its ingrained memory of the road. Now, I do not worry about such things happening. I can even feel my legs, pumping away. I sense them in a mode that's different from ordinary perception, but it's perception just the same. Then, I focus on my hands and make pale, almost bloodless fingers clutch the *dee-da* tighter.

I suddenly feel more confident than I have in ages. I can overcome any adversity; I just gotta get my head in the race. That's what Coach de Papa always told me. It won't be easy, being decapitated and all, but I'm up for the challenge— *always* up for the challenge.

If it can be done, then Oscar Legbo can do it.

Helmut Starb:

Helmut's bliss became confusion. Oscar's body refused to fall from the bike, and—weirder still—his feet refused to stop manipulating the pedals.

He wondered how he would have reacted if it'd been his head instead of Oscar's. Would he have kept going like a trooper or shat his pants and fell to the road, twitching and dead?

This made him hate Oscar all the more.

He drew in a few deep breaths, but they did nothing to calm him. He had to slow down, to process everything that he'd seen and was seeing. No rider was close to him yet; he remained comfortably in second place, and Oscar had to fall *sometime* before the finish line; the race had over 40 miles to go.

The slower pace did relax him somewhat, and it helped to be farther away from Oscar, to not see the blood geyser, his ragged neck, and the little sprig of spine that sprouted from it.

Soon, he heard the *whizzz* of an approaching bike. Someone was gaining on him. He turned around and saw that it was Decker, who slowed down as he approached Helmut.

"Oh God!" Decker shouted, looking at Oscar, who was, from his perspective, a red-spurting dot. "What happened?"

"Some ninja guy cut off Oscar Legbo's head!"

"A ninja guy?"

Helmut nodded.

"Then why's Oscar still in the race?"

"Fuck if I know!"

Decker turned around to face the road and pumped his legs faster. Helmut did likewise, but the Belgian still managed to slip ahead of him.

I don't think I like that guy anymore, Helmut thought.

Ninja:

I lose myself in birdsongs and the sound of the gently babbling stream—then my goddamned head starts buzzing again: *"You must commit* Hiri-kuku!" The voice shouts. *"Do it now!"*

"What!" I say, aloud this time. "That wasn't part of the agreement!"

"Oh, yes it was. You just don't remember."

I cup my face into my hands; I want to live. Still, *Hiri-kuku* provides the noblest way out for a ninja, and all flesh—I remind myself—must rot away eventually.

Hiri-kuku is accomplished by cramming three large sweet potatoes down ones throat until one chokes to death. Too bad I don't have sweet potatoes handy, but my socks are orange and perhaps they'll suffice. Too bad there're only two of them; guess I'll also have to use my underwear.

I bend down, and, with a heavy yet willing heart, remove my black ninja slippers and pull off my bright orange tube socks.

Bright orange tube socks?

I stare at them, again confused. Shouldn't I be wearing silky ninja stockings? But these socks have different colored bands printed around their tops, like something an 80s kid would wear.

No matter. I rip them from my feet and stuff them, reeking, into my mouth. (*Are ninja feet supposed to reek? Fuck it.*) Then I remove my sleek ninja pants and see that I'm wearing tighty whities beneath them, and that my legs and thighs are flabby and pasty, like those of an overweight, thirty-something American.

But why would I have this sword and mask if I were not a ninja? I didn't see other people dressed up today. It's certainly not Halloween.

My head starts buzzing again. When the voice speaks, it's positively screaming.

"Ninjas don't know about Halloween, you dumb ass."

I spit the socks from my mouth. "Shut up!"

"It's a western thing."

"I know! I know!"

"So, if you know this, then you also know there's no way you're a ninja from 16th century Japan."

"Fuck you, fuck you, I am a ninja! Fuck you!"

I run behind a tree and beat my head upon nurturing and life-giving ground. When the voices finally stop, my forehead is lacerated and there are twigs in my mask.

In the Channel 5 Newsroom:

Anchorlady Jane: If you are just joining us, Oscar Legbo has not only again proved his stamina and virility by racing without a head, but has also provided the world with a truly unique and amazing moment in sports.

Anchorman Tim: *Amazing* is not the word. Try *ball-staggering*, Jane.

Anchorlady Jane: Why don't I just stick with *amazing*? At any rate, what was once national mourning has become national hope. If Oscar Legbo manages to pull through, not only will he win his eighth *Tour de Saucisse-Dommages*, but he'll also become the first rider to do so while decapitated.

Anchorman Tim: Keep in mind that he has over twenty miles to go before he reaches the finish line.

Anchorlady Jane: If past performance is any indicator, then Oscar Legbo should have no problem.

Anchorman Tim (*bites his bottom lip*): But he had a frickin' head then, woman! Sheesh! (*Draws in a deep, calming breath.*) But if anyone is capable of pulling off such a feat, it's Oscar Legbo.

Anchorlady Jane: And now we go to roving reporter Jake Dallas for another edition of *The Word on the Street.*

(*Cuts to a heavyset young man, standing with a microphone on the corner of a busy city street.*)

Jake Dallas: Thank you, Jane. (*He approaches a smart looking woman in a business suit.*) What do you think Oscar's chances are of winning this year's *Tour de Saucisse-Dommages*?

Woman: He'll win. I have faith in Oscar, and think he'll do America proud next year, too.

Jake Dallas: You think he'll be in next year's race, too?

Woman: Yes.

Jake Dallas (*approaches a middle-aged man in a ball cap and wife-beater*): And how about you, sir? Do you think Oscar Legbo still has what it takes to win?

Man (*speaks while crushing a beer can against his crotch*): Whew fuckin' hoo! A-frikin'merica, baby!

Jake Dallas: I guess that means yes. (*He faces the camera.*)

So, as you can see, the American public believes Oscar Legbo has what it takes to win this race—and perhaps future races —even without a head.

(Cut from Jake Dallas to a live shot of the Tour de Saucisse-Dommages. *Oscar's body is seen, pumping the pedals and controlling the handlebar in such a way that if one were to put a sheet of paper on the television where his head used to be and ignore all the blood on his clothes and bike, one would think that things were still par for the course.)*

<u>Anchorlady Jane</u> (voice-over): The blood geyser is still flowing, I had no idea a man could have that much gore in him, but I no longer see it as a disgusting thing. I now think of it as a red *Fountain of Freedom.*

<u>Anchorman Tim</u> (voice-over): That's very touching, Jane. I'm sorry I said all those bad things about you earlier.

(Live feed ends.)

Helmut Starb:

Walri Power Go! He thought, and allowed the strength of the *Odobenus rosmarus* to become his own. Helmut pedaled harder and harder until he was right on Decker's tail.

But, as it so happened, he didn't need the extra get-up-and-go because Decker had slowed down considerably. Once neck-and-neck with Oscar, he now trailed him by at least twenty feet.

Helmut swerved to his left, maneuvering his bike so that it traveled alongside the Belgian's. He shouted: "I don't care if you or I win, just as long as one of us beats Legbo! It's now or—"

Helmut froze. Decker sported the largest boner he had ever seen.

"What the—what the hell are you thinking about?"

The Belgian didn't respond immediately. His eyes didn't even seem to be looking at anything in this world, though they were focused on the red geyser still shooting miraculously from Legbo's neck stump.

"Oh god! Oh god, it's so beautiful!"

"What? *That's* giving you a hard-on?" Helmut crinkled his nose; a fan of Oscar's blood had gotten on the man's

BAG WORM
a poem by Oscar Legbo

I want to live in a house
just like yours.
Knit one for me, please.
Knit it with love
in a pine tree

but stay clear
of the bottom branches
where it might get picked
by uncaring hands.

pants. "It's not sexy, it's disgusting. And you're a sick fuck, Decker."

"No, not *it*," he moaned. "Look *into* it and see!"

"Excuse me?"

"The *things*—the beautiful twisty golden spirals of eternal agape love! See them!"

"Eternal agape what?"

"LOVE!" Decker screamed, eyes bulging so far that Helmut feared they might shoot out and hit him. Then he noticed thin wisps of smoke rising from Decker's ears and his slightly parted mouth.

"Are you okay?" Helmut shouted, his confusion making him say the first thing that came to mind. "Do you need an antacid or something?"

Instead of replying, the Belgian burst into flames.

Ninja:

I've never felt lower or more dejected in my life—but I am *Ninja*; this I must believe. It's the core of my being, my *Upbranahamanan*, my uppermost soul. Evidence to the contrary shall not sway me. I don't care if a million screaming cops descend upon me in Messerschmitt fashion and have me locked in a padded room where I receive Thorazine and enemas for the remainder of my days. These things are *mayanamanana*, illusion. Sweet and green Japanese fields will always be my home, but even they too are illusion. The only thing that is real is me…

… and I am *Ninja*.

Inside Oscar's severed head:

I feel someone try to pick up my head and, judging from the sound of rustling plastic, put it in a bag. I don't know if it's a paramedic or a souvenir seeker, and I don't care either way.

"Leave me alone! I'm fucking trying to concentrate here!" I manage to groan, the sound like water gurgling through a leaf-clogged drain.

The man runs away, screaming.

That particular distraction is gone, but another follows, and it's far more difficult to ignore or brush off. The bugs have returned; I imagine that they are huge and I am tiny, and I am lost in their world. Once again, I am connected to a body, but, if I could, I'd wish it away. Angry souls surround it, bite at it, stomp-tickle it with bristly feet.

"Please stop," I shout at them. "Please leave me alone and let me do what I have to do!"

"You didn't leave us alone, Mr. Legbo," they say, their voice a collective one, high-pitched and nearly sonic. "So why should we leave you alone?"

"Haven't I done enough? Haven't I atoned?"

"You can never atone, not in our eyes, eyes which once saw and enjoyed the world, but no longer."

"I need to win. That's all I ask of you. Let me win this race, please."

"That's not possible. You belong to us, and it's only fitting that you do."

"But I wear your image on my uniform! My severed head has plastic antennae stuck to it! Don't these things count?"

"No."

Rage like I hadn't felt in years builds up inside. "Well, fuck you, then! I was silly for loving you, for caring that I killed you! You're just bugs for Christ's sake! I'm going to win this race and I'm going to do it without you!"

The bug spirits waver and hitch as though their forms have become quicksilver on a hot city street. When they are gone, Coach de Papa appears before me, glistening. Shirtless, he wears the same tiny pair of red running shorts that I've grown to know and love. His look is rugged, and a moustache stretches across the entirety of his aged yet joyful face.

Still, his gaze seems far off: "Oscar, I am so proud."

I can barely speak. "Coach—Coach de Papa is that you?"

"Of course, Oscar."

"But you're dead."

"And you—for all intents and purposes—are, too."

He has a point. "But why are you here? And why are you proud?"

"Because you finally got off your bug kick, that's why. I wish you knew how much it pained me to see such a talented man live his life with such a silly, silly burden. You went far in that life, but you could have gone farther had you been free." Coach de Papa pauses to flex, his seventy-six year old body firm and taut. "Too bad you had to lose your head before you realized this, but that's the way the world works sometimes."

"Yes, Coach de Papa, I know."

"But you were always stubborn, and you marched to the sound of your own drum, for good or for ill." His eyes sparkle. "And that's why I always admired you, even if that admiration was begrudging at times."

"But I killed you, Coach de Papa."

"I don't worry about that anymore."

I look down at my imaginary feet. "You seemed so angry before you died."

"You're sure as shit I was angry. I didn't want to be messed with, not then. You could have talked to me, that would have been fine, but you had to go and mess with the trident."

"But I couldn't just watch you die."

"Would you want someone messing with a trident if every time he touched it your entire body rippled with pain?"

"No, Coach de Papa. I wouldn't, and I'm sorry."

"I know you're sorry; you have a good heart." My coach offers a thin smile. "Come to think of it, you remind me of myself at your age, only more gay."

I feel as though someone has punched me. "What!"

He moves in closer and lays a big, thick hand down on my imaginary shoulder. "Be true to yourself, Oscar."

"I—I don't know what to say, Papa."

"Perhaps this the best—if not only—time to figure out what to say." He shakes his head. "You can be the world's greatest bicycle racer and be gay at the same time, you know."

Events that I had forgotten suddenly flood back and, once the pieces come together, they make sense: The times

I'd watch Coach de Papa from the corner of my eye in the changing room, the day I pantsed him playfully, but really wanted to see if he wore anything beneath his shorts (which he didn't), and the fact that I masturbated to his picture not once but twice.

"Yes, Papa," I finally say. "Yes, I see. And while I don't admit that I was gay, I admit that I was gay for you."

"That's enough for me, Oscar. Good boy." He rakes his hands across my imaginary chest and shakes away sweat. "That's what I've always wanted to hear."

"It is?"

"Yes, now stop obsessing. Clear your mind and do what needs to be done. Focus. Get your head in the race. Okay?"

"I will, Coach de Papa."

"Win for me. Fuck a bunch of bugs."

"I will, on both counts."

He turns away. "I gotta go now. My time here is through."

"Okay, but it was good seeing you again."

"You, too."

"Goodbye, Coach."

"Goodbye, Oscar." He smiles—widely and warmly, just the way I remember—and then he's gone.

Suddenly, I'm back on the ground, eyes closed and focusing again on the race. I feel that the antennae have slid from my head, and it's a good thing.

My head is in the race like never before.

Helmut Starb:

Helmut fell back and made sure not to stare directly into the red fountain spurting from Oscar's neck. If the Belgian could spontaneously combust, then he figured the same could happen to him.

Pierre LaChaise, the Frenchman, took advantage of this opportunity and passed Helmut without a backwards glance.

At that moment, he decided he didn't much like that guy anymore, either.

Ninja:

The voice in my head: *We're really happy that you feel good about yourself and all, but it's time for* Hiri-kuku *now. Please, do not keep us waiting.*

The buzz that accompanies this voice no longer bothers me, for I now know what I have to do, and have come to terms with it. I delay no longer. I pick up my tube socks without dusting them off. I put them in my mouth, along with my briefs, but cannot swallow these things enough to choke.

I must use a stick, so I take one from the ground beside me and ram it against the wad in my throat until my hands are raw and bloody. The briefs remain stuck to the back of my throat, but the socks, I imagine, are far enough down to get the job done. My skin is sweaty; I cannot breathe, and my heart races. Ninja training had covered *Hiri-kuku*, but it did nothing to prepare me for the actual experience.

I must relax; I cannot freak out.

Once again, my head buzzes: "*A ninja does not use the term 'freak out'.*"

"Shut up!" I think-scream. "I'm trying to die here!"

The voice falls mercifully silent. I collapse into a

carpet of leaves. Bringing my hands to my face, I see that they are blue. When I bring them down, a great vortex spins before me, growing wider by the second.

I say in my head: *Oh sweet* Brumahumananan, *or whatever god Ninjas worship—provided I am, in fact, a ninja and not some overweight thirty-nine year old trucker named Joe—protect me as I pass from this world and enter the next*!

The pain goes away. The world for which I'd prayed opens before me, and it no longer matters whether I'm a ninja or not. All that matters is that I visualize myself amongst the corky, twisty trees of the orient, thinking, oddly enough, of a particularly tasty hamburger I'd eaten at a Tulsa, Oklahoma rest stop in 1992.

Inside Oscar's severed head:

Just when I think I'm going to make it, a pleasant haze washes over my brain. It's tempting, and I want to fall headlong into it, but I must hold out. I haven't gone this far just to stop. I didn't beat the bugs and express undying love for my dead coach to collapse before reaching the finish.

But I can no longer feel my legs, and can only barely feel my hands. I see them with my mind's eye, still confidently pumping away and gripping, but don't know how long they can maintain such efficiency without 100% of my essence there to guide them.

Focusing on my body is now useless, so I pan my gaze out in front of me, to the road as it unfurls. I'm familiar with this stretch as I'm familiar with all stretches along the *Tour de Saucisse-Dommages*. There's only a mile to go, give or take, but that upstart Frenchman is neck-and-neck with me.

It's almost as though he senses my scrutiny as he turns to my body and extends his middle finger while laughing. Has he no respect for the dead?

In the Channel 5 Newsroom:

<u>Anchorlady Jane</u>: I've just received word that a rider—#4, Pierre LaChaise from Catrombeau, France—is gaining on Oscar and may just take the lead.

<u>Anchorman Tim</u> (*slams fists on desk until knuckles bleed*): Goddamn that asshole! I hope he breaks his neck!

(Cut to live news-feed from the Tour de Saucisse-Dommages. *Pierre LaChaise vies with Oscar Legbo for the lead. He smirks confidently as he taunts Legbo, but that confident look turns to one of sudden terror. His eyes grow wide and a pained expression spreads across his face. Then he collapses against the handlebars. Seconds later, the bicycle goes over a ravine, immediately after which the scene cuts back to the news desk.)*

<u>Anchorlady Jane</u>: It appears as though Pierre LaChaise has suffered a heart attack and may, in fact, be dead. Unless something major happens, Oscar Legbo will surely win the last stage of the *Tour de Saucisse-Dommages*.

<u>Anchorman Tim</u>: Yes! Go, Legbo, go!

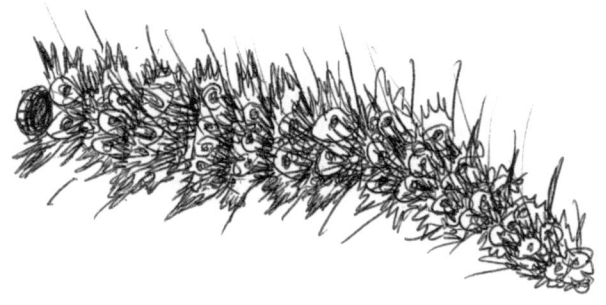

FUZZY CATERPILLAR

a poem by Oscar Legbo

If you could remove
your fuzz like a coat
would you let me
borrow it?

Would you let me cover
my horrible man skin
and become you
for a day?

Meanwhile, as all this is taking place:

The CEO of *Legbo International* paced across an oak and marble boardroom as he rethought his global strategy. Two other men were in attendance, seated at a long, rectangular table in an otherwise empty room.

"I want to ask you"—the CEO stopped pacing—"if it's possible to effectively market a headless role model."

A sycophant: "I don't see why not."

"Won't the T-shirts appear distasteful?"

"Perhaps, but I've heard that kids go for gore."

"Really?"

The sycophant nodded.

The CEO resumed pacing. "Of course, we'll have to revise our action figure line, too. And we'll have to do more than just remove their heads. Something else needs to be done, something that will give them extra added *oomph*."

"Excuse me, sir, but could they have super squirting action?"

The CEO spent a few moments in thought. Then: "I *love* that idea."

The third wheel: "And you'd need the liquid inside to be red, of course."

"Of course," the sycophant replied. "Do you think we're idiots?"

"No sir. I do most certainly *not* think—under any set of possible circumstances—that anyone in this room today is an idiot."

The CEO leered. "Are you sure about that?"

"Yes, sir!"

The sycophant turned to the other man. "Personally, I'm not so sure."

The CEO laughed.

The third wheel sulked.

Ninja:

I come to and realize what I'd seen wasn't ninja heaven at all. I was just suffering from delusions brought on by panic and a lack of oxygen. Also, the socks and briefs have slipped from my throat and out of my mouth before they could choke me to death.

My head starts buzzing, louder than ever. "*What kind of fucking ninja are you? You can't even commit* hiri-kuku!"

I get up, slowly. "I—I'm sorry. I am a bad ninja and, through my failings, have brought a great and everlasting shame down upon my head."

"*You can say that again.*"

I say that again; then sigh and bend down to retrieve my clothing. I put the socks and underwear back on, unnerved to feel their wet stickiness against my skin, but they're all I've got, so they must suffice. Then I slip the bottom half of my ninja gear back on, but wearing it feels wrong, as I may no longer be worthy of the honor.

"*You're not, so hold your breath until you die.*"

There is too much inner feedback for me to hear: "What?"

"*I said hold your breath until you die!*"

I try this, but each time my heart starts racing and my face starts turning blue, I exhale with a gush.

"*You're not supposed to start breathing again! That's the whole point!*"

"But it hurts if I don't breathe!"

"*Of course it hurts! It's supposed to kill you, you dumb ass!*"

"Please, give me another way out!"

"*Okay, then. Why don't you swallow your tongue?*"

"But that is a *very* dishonorable way for a ninja to die! It will bring shame not only to me, but to my entire community!"

"*Do it anyway!*"

And so I do, but, again, it fails to work; my tongue just isn't long enough.

The buzzing is now so loud I fear I might go deaf. "*We hoped it wouldn't come to this, but you give us no choice. For failing three times, you must be punished.*"

I steel myself, apprehensive yet nevertheless ready to accept the punishment, for I know, in my broken ninja heart, that I deserve whatever I get.

The shouted commands begin:

"*Bop yourself in the head!*"

I bop myself in the head.

"*Stick your fingers in your eyes!*"

I stick my fingers in my eyes.

"*Say you're a stupid, fairy pansy muthafucka!*"

"I am a stupid, fairy pansy muthafucka."

Another voice, usually there's only one: "*Stop it! Now you're just playing with him.*"

"*Sorry. Where was I?*"

"You were punishing me, sir."

"Yes, yes. That's right. Well, we're finished with that."

"Now that I've been punished, can I go on with my life and not commit *hiri-kuku*?"

"No," the voice again roars. *"Commit* hiri-kuku! *How many times do we have to fucking say it?"*

I don't know what to do, so I look around for things that, if used correctly, might prove deadly. First, I try to drown myself in the creek, but it's the same as holding my breath; each time it starts to hurt, I stop. Then, I poke at myself with a stick for fifteen minutes, but it does nothing but irritate my skin. Later, I find a long, green garden snake and try to strangle myself with it, but it bites me and I scream and the thing slithers away.

I try everything in the woods, but nothing there will kill me, or maybe it's that everything around me *is* lethal, but I just don't have the balls to make anything *be* lethal.

"You're fucking hopeless; do you know that?"

"Yes," I say. "Yes, I know."

In the Channel 5 Newsroom:

<u>Anchorlady Jane</u> (*unfastens the top two buttons on her blouse*): Well, it looks like I've come down with Legbo Fever tonight.

<u>Anchorman Tim</u>: That doesn't make you special, Jane. The whole country has Legbo Fever.

<u>Anchorlady Jane</u> (*quickly refastens the top two buttons*): You might be right, Tim. At any rate, this is a glorious day for America.

<u>Anchorman Tim</u>: Better than Christmas, the Fourth of July, and a good Tijuana lay, all wrapped into one.

<u>Anchorlady Jane</u>: I wouldn't know about Tijuana lays, but—

<u>Anchorman Tim</u> (*appears as though he might be masturbating behind his desk*): Take a look at this! Can you believe it, Jane? Oh shit! Oh holy shit! Yes! *Yes*! It looks like Oscar Lego is just seconds away from winning his eighth *Tour de Saucisse-Dommages*!

Inside Oscar's severed head:

I feel bad for what happened to the Frenchman. He was an asshole, but didn't deserve to die. I didn't even know that I could do that. I just projected my anger at him—in the most dark, horrible and drippy corpse-like form I could muster— and hoped he might sense the presence and feel a vague sense of unease. I didn't expect that he would actually see the thought-form and *die*.

But oh well…

With the Frenchman gone, the end is in sight. Ordinarily, I'd feel very comfortable at this point in the race, but now I feel less certain, the prospect of making it all the way no longer guaranteed. Everything is dark and fuzzy before it goes over to gray, then black.

Helmut Starb:

Fuck it. If I spontaneously combust or fall off a cliff, just fuck it. I'll win this race if it kills me.

Helmut concentrated on his skullcap and there found the strength to pump the pedals with *pinnipedal power*—(At that moment, he reminded himself that he should have the phrase 'pinnipedal power' trademarked as quickly as possible)—and, in a matter of seconds, caught sight of Legbo.

"You're mine, bugfucker!" He moved in to usurp the lead, so close now that Oscar's blood splashed on him, turning his white and blue racing uniform red. Helmut found himself enjoying, if not luxuriating in, the hot and sticky warmth, and wondering if this made him a freak.

But the sensation, he soon discovered, wasn't erotic at all. The blood was doing something to him—perhaps on a molecular level—and reminding him of the time he dropped acid at college in Frankfurt.

Maybe, he thought, *I should let Oscar win.*

Then: *What am I thinking?*

And then: *Oscar deserves it; Oscar is great and bugs are great. Better than walri.*

Finally: *No they're not—but they are! Oh God, they are!*

Against his will, Helmut looked deeply into the Fountain of Freedom, past the apparent and into the *real*. What he saw scrubbed his mind, and he could only think, *it's love; it's all love* over and over again. Physically, his hair stood on end; his walri skullcap tumbled off his scalp, and his phallus extended so fast and furiously that the boner snapped his tiny Euro briefs.

Something bubbled inside him; he broke into a sweat that was first hot then cold. Helmut couldn't see his ears, but he knew smoke rose from them. If he didn't release energy soon he would combust, so he jumped off the bike and tore a hole in his racing uniform right over the crotch. Then he got facedown on the road, arched his back, and, with his right hand—and in front of an audience of millions—saved himself from a fiery demise.

No one at the race or in the viewing audience paid much attention, however. All eyes were turned to Legbo, his Fountain of Freedom shooting higher than ever as he crossed the finish line in first place.

Inside Oscar's severed head:

I sense that I have crossed the finish line, but have no way of knowing this. Also, I have no way of knowing how much time has passed, for the void that now wants me seems timeless. No matter. Such things are no longer in my realm of concern. I've done what I needed to get done; now I can rest.

At the very last second, my perception returns, like a personal slideshow that I'm able to tune into from afar. My headless corpse is now being carried, held aloft by countless loving hands.

I also sense that my working has been successful; I feel a presence around me now, one that I've never felt outside the meditative state. Still, I don't know how long the working can be sustained without me around to guide and nurture it; I fear it will fade as I do, but maybe a taste of agape love is all the world needs to satiate itself.

I want to smile, but cannot. I couldn't have asked for a better scene with which to end my life, so I allow my inner eyes to close. As my mind begins to unfurl, I again scream out to the only man I have ever loved.

Coach de Papa, Coach de Papa, be my guru and

infuse meaning into my soul. In my last thought, as a gift to you, I will think of a dee-da *as a handlebar. That was another thing you always wanted, and I know this now. Coach de Papa, Coach de Papa—forgive me for my blindness, and, most of all, forgive me for killing you when I should have squashed the bug.*

His voice returns, booming in my head: "I forgive you, son."

He called me 'son.' I can die now. I can die. I die.
Where am I?

The Outpouring:

(So many reports and updates have come into the studio since Oscar's victory that <u>Anchorman Tim</u> *has had no time to celebrate. Stagehands constantly cycle by the desk, throwing small white notes onto it. The surface is covered, but they throw still more. Both anchors scramble to keep up with the influx, but are drowning.)*

<u>Anchorlady Jane</u> *(passes out briefly, unable to withstand the volume of reports, updates, and newsflashes).*

<u>Anchorman Tim</u> *(pauses to catch his breath)*: This is truly the greatest fucking moment in sports.

<u>Anchorlady Jane</u> *(lifts head briefly to read from a note, and then drops it again)*: Yes, Tim. People are spontaneously combusting. Fire is everywhere, but the fire is said to be beautiful beyond words.

<u>Anchorman Tim</u>: And for every person on fire there is another masturbating in public, but no one cares because even the

police are doing it.

Anchorlady Jane (*arises and picks up a report littered with pie charts and diagrams*): And it is predicted that, twenty years from now, Oscar will be the legal name of approximately 876,040,530 people worldwide.

Anchorman Tim: Also, the CDC has declared Legbo Fever to be the first ever *epidemic of joy*.

Anchorlady Jane (*picks up yet another note, appearing to have been rendered in orange crayon*): A litter of alien atomic kittens (or AAK, for short) was discovered wrapped up in a basket near Hyde Park today. It is unknown whether these creatures were alive or dead at the time of their discovery. We will keep you updated as to how this story develops.

Anchorman Tim (*is handed another sheet of paper, but this time the stagehand shoves it directly in his face, like it's very, very important and must be read* now): This just in: there is no more war; there is no more famine, and the dead are no longer dead. Rejoice, America; your loved ones return!

Anchorlady Jane (*receives her own urgent message and reads it on-air*): Crackbabies are no longer crackbabies!

Anchorman Tim: The national debt has vanished!

Anchorlady Jane: And hospitals and mortuaries have closed

down!

Anchorman Tim (*sweeps notes to the floor; gets atop the desk and rends his clothing*): There is nothing but love, shooting, spurting gouts of effervescent love, covering the nation—in *love*.

(Anchorman Tim *and* Anchorlady Jane *lose focus. They dart their eyes about the studio and swat their arms around in the air as though fending off something that the viewing audience cannot see.*)

Anchorlady Jane: It's too big, too big and righteous. I can't let it into my body!

Anchorman Tim: It's too strong, Jane! You can't fight it!

(*Nevertheless, they continue to fight for another minute, after which time they finally give in to the moment. Violent seizures rock their bodies; their eyes roll in ecstasy. Minutes pass before* Anchorman Tim *and* Anchorlady Jane *regain consciousness. When they do, their eyes look different, glassy.*)

Anchorlady Jane (*turns to Anchorman Tim*): I want you inside me.

Anchorman Tim: You're already there.

Anchorlady Jane: Am I?

Anchorman Tim: Yes.

Anchorlady Jane: And have I always been there—(*pupils dilate suddenly*)—coiling inside your soul?

Anchorman Tim: Yes.

Anchorlady Jane (*looks at her hands*): Am I tripping out?

Anchorman Tim: Relax. Just go with the flow.

Anchorlady Jane: Am I going to die, Tim?

Anchorman Tim: No Jane, you're going to live.

Anchorlady Jane (*goes with the flow*): I am Love, Tim.

Anchorman Tim: And I am Love, Jane.

(*They lift their hands and touch their palms together and stare into each other's eyes.*)

Anchormanlady Timjane: We now are Linked; we are United; we are One. God is with us. We are with God. God is with us. We are with God.

(*They repeat these two lines twenty-five times before saying anything new.*)

Anchorladyman Janetim: It is *void* that I see; it is Nirvana. We are here. Radiate with us. Radiate with our splendor.

(*They babble for fifteen minutes before falling silent. With vacant expressions, they stare at and into the camera for another fifteen, sometimes reaching arms out as though to touch something. No one in the studio cares, nor does anyone in the home audience, either, because they're all doing the same thing.*)

The Ultimate End:

The crowd at the finish line carried Oscar's body for nearly ten minutes, hooting, hollering, and enveloped by the sheer joy that was Legbo. They imagined they carried him not on the ground, but in space, atop a blanket of exploding, Technicolor stars. By the time they dropped him by the winner's platform, the hallucinations had ended, and the red *Fountain of Freedom* had gone dry.

Still, the press corps gathered around a now garland and tinsel draped Legbo, often having their pictures made with him or contorting his body into suggestive or alluring poses. Someone else shook a bottle of champagne, opened it, and, in the spirit of celebration, sprayed its contents all over Legbo. Yet another approached Oscar and rubbed his hands up and down his cold chest and, in an entirely different spirit, groped Legbo's package repeatedly. No one stopped the man from doing this, so quite a few others soon joined in.

"Speech! Speech!" someone said.

But Oscar made no speech.

Everyone waited for him to get up, thinking, perhaps,

that he was just tired from the race, but he never did.

When realization set in, hooting and hollering turned into lunging and slobbering.

In the Channel 5 Newsroom:

Anchorman Tim (*sits with his head on the desk and his fingers laced in his hair, down from his sudden agape love high and feeling very hung over. Just seconds earlier he had been animated, coming out of his love trance and spraying various fluids all over the newsroom and the people in it. When he finally speaks, his voice sounds lifeless*): It's now official; Oscar Lebgo is completely and utterly *dead.*

Anchorlady Jane (*feels separation anxiety due to her sudden soul-split with Tim, but maintains composure for the camera's sake, though her bra still hangs half-on/half-off the desk*): That's true, and it's also been reported that numerous fights have broken out amongst the crowd at the *Tour de Saucisse-Dommages*. It is uncertain at this moment whether fatalities are involved, but I've been told that these skirmishes are especially brutal and involve most, if not all, of the spectators.

Anchorman Tim: Whoop de shit.

Back in the Boardroom:

"Damn it! Damn it all!" The CEO of *Legbo International* reached into a desk drawer and removed a box of capsules. "I never thought it would come to this." He turned to the sycophant. "Give one capsule to every worker here today, and then take one yourself."

The sycophant arose from his chair and gave a salute. "Yes, sir!"

"Good. Now take the box; do what you have to do."

The sycophant disappeared quickly from the office, box in hand.

"And you"—he turned to the third wheel—"I want you on corpse detail, and don't forget to take *your* pill afterwards."

"Must I?"

"Of course; you know the drill." The CEO smiled. "And I'm taking mine last just to make sure you take yours first."

Ninja:

As much as I might want to, I cannot stay here. If I cannot die, then I must return home and face the wrath of my community. But then I realize that I don't know where home is or if I'm even part of a community.

And what will I do once I get wherever it is I'm going? What *can* a one-time ninja do in the real world? Work fast food? Wash cars? It's not as though I have money to go back to college.

My answer is suddenly clear: I must become a wanderer; I will have no brothers or sisters, and a staff will be my constant companion.

* * * *

I walk for almost twenty minutes before I again hear the sounds of chaos. Instead of dying down, the noises have intensified.

As I begin to see the road, I realize things are hanging from the trees that line it. I can't see what they are until I get closer: people dangling without pants, for their pants now serve as both ropes and hangman's nooses. A few of the bodies twitch, though most are still.

I wonder what caused this, and then hope that whatever did wouldn't cause the same to happen to me, especially since I'm wearing tighty whities and would hate to be caught dead in them.

But I am *Ninja*; I must be strong; I must ready myself for any possible assault against me. In preparation, I reach down deep to locate my chi, but it's nowhere to be found.

I exit the woods anyway, and then enter into madness. At first I think monsters are ripping at each other with teeth and hands like claws. Then I realize these monsters possess human forms, which makes me think they're zombies—or, as we ninjas call them, *gualangas*—but the absence of decaying flesh tells me this cannot be so.

An ugly, misshapen man passes close by, though he does not turn in my direction. It takes some time for me to realize that this isn't a man at all, but a woman wearing a freshly shorn skin suit.

Then a voice interrupts my thoughts, but it's not in my head: "Hey, ninja-man," a young, crew cut guy in an Oscar Legbo t-shirt mumbles as he lurches towards me, something hanging from his mouth that looks suspiciously like a severed penis. "Wanna *rumble-ahhaha* with me?"

I do not know what this person is talking about, so I say nothing.

He gets closer. Now I see that the thing is undoubtedly a penis and, judging by the growing red stain on his pants, it's his own. "I said, do you want to *rumble-ahhaha*?"

This man won't leave me alone, so I humor him: "I'll

gladly *rumble-ahhaha* with you, provided the taste of my sword is to your liking."

I look down, and realize that I've left my sword in the woods. "*Fuck*," I say under my breath and run away, but barely go two steps before encountering another bunch of crazies. These bastards are all committing variations of *hiri-kuku*, successfully, and in mass numbers. And they aren't even ninjas, just stupid flabby Americans and Europeans. I hate them. I hate them so much.

My head buzzes: "*Face it, you're just jealous because they can commit* hiri-kuku *and you can't!*"

And it is then that I realize—truly realize—that the voices in my head have always been right, and that I do suck —and suck hard—as a ninja.

In the Channel 5 Newsroom:

Anchorlady Jane: And we again go live to reporter Jake Dallas for perhaps the most important segment of *The Word on the Street* ever.

(*Cuts to the same heavyset young man, standing with a microphone on the corner of the same city street.*)

Jake Dallas: What do you think our chances are of surviving until tomorrow?

Man #1 (*dressed like a TV repairman*): Slim to none. The Fuck Apocalypse has arrived. It's so bad outside now that all we can do is go inside and fuck.

Jake Dallas: I guess you better get going, then. Sorry to keep you. (*Turns from the man and approaches a woman dressed as a bohemian poet.*) Now, I'd like to ask you that same question.

Woman: It's all death and death and gray and gray. It's all thunderstorms, cloudbursts, and rainy days.

Jake Dallas: Indeed, and how about you, sir?

Man #2 *(dressed like a total retard)*: We're totally plungered, dude.

Jake Dallas: And you? (*Turns to a man dressed head to toe in entrails. Otherwise, he is naked.*)

Man #3: Skidee-haha! Skidau alpo-mennyhanah! Skidoo delap-nahanaha! (*He attempts to lick Jake Dallas, his hands leaving deep red stains on the reporter's suit as he clutches it.*)

Jake Dallas: Please, you're upsetting me, and need to back away.

Man #3 (*rediscovers his human tongue*): You didn't say 'the fuck.'

Jake Dallas: Excuse me?

Man #3: For me to have taken you seriously, you should have said 'and need to back *the fuck* away.'

Jake Dallas: I'm sorry. Can I—say it again?

Man #3: No, too late! Skidaa hoffa-nomenklatta! I'm going to rip your heart out with my teeth! (*Then he does just that.*)

(*Cut to the news desk at Channel 5.*)

Anchorlady Jane: We hope the best for Jake Dallas.

Anchorman Tim: Fuck him. (*He leaves his desk with a lumbering gate.*) And fuck everything else for that matter.

Anchorlady Jane (*is very confused*): Well, I guess the show has to—uh… wait, I'm receiving word that people—perhaps hundreds of them—are throwing things at our downtown office.

(*A blood-leaking stagehand staggers up to Jane and hands her a note before collapsing.*)

Anchorlady Jane: Oh, my God, if what I'm reading is true, then that man Jake interviewed was right. The Fuck Apocalypse has arrived as people—if I can even call them that—throw severed human heads and various other freshly carved parts at our downtown office. Please stop doing this. Please stop rioting. No sports figure is worth a single life lost. I'd even say no god is worth it. Please stop. There have been reports of cannibalism. Don't do this. Please go home now; tend to your families. (*Her eyes widen and her mouth becomes a wide O.*) Oh my God, Tim!

(**Anchorman Tim** *is presently off camera, biting an unresponsive stagehand. Then he chows down, ripping away and then consuming half the man's face in a single bite. Tim notices her attention and lunges in her direction, a piece of gristle hanging over his bottom lip.*)

Anchorlady Jane (*Spoken off camera, while running*): And

now we go live to an emergency address from the President!

(*Cut to the President, again sitting in a chair in the oval office. He too appears to have something hanging over his lip.*)

<u>President</u>: Oh Glory *Hallelujanamarah*—or however you people out there say it—we, as a nation, have gone from the heights of expectation to the heights of sorrow to the heights of joy and back again in a single day. Oh *God-Narharmarhar*—this is too much for us, myself included, to take.

My Fellow Americans, we have long feared its arrival, but *Apocalypse Fuck* is finally here.

Intersplice: **The Office of Standards and Practices** would do something, provided people there weren't busy fucking and/or killing each other.

President (*cont.*):

Fellow nations, please don't look down on Americans or America as a whole; you can't expect us *not* to break down, to break down and cry, if not scream and rend things, breaking the intact and annihilating the already broken; nor can we be expected not to put things in our mouths or other cavities that were never intended for such ingress, or not to run naked and screaming through the dark and sticky passageways of a night that will never end.

I'm sorry—so terribly sorry—but there's no magic pill to swallow that will return us to our previous state. It is a paradise lost. And so—beginning with this proclamation—Oscar Legbo supplants the eagle to become America's new symbol, one that our beautiful dead and dying nation can get behind as it takes that great and final leap into the Forever Beyond.

Ladies and gentleman, I've said all that I can say, and now must leave you. (*President removes a small caliber revolver from his coat and blows his brains out on national TV.*)

(*Cut back to the newsroom, but there's no one there, and the camera is slightly askew.*)

ABOUT THE AUTHOR

Kevin lives in the hills of Tennessee.

His short fiction and poetry has appeared in such venues as The Mammoth Book of Legal Thrillers, Flesh and Blood, ChiZine, The Cafe Irreal, Poe's Progeny, Book of Dark Wisdom, Dark Discoveries, Bathtub Gin, Not One of Us, Dreams and Nightmares, Electric Velocipede, Sick: An Anthology of Illness, Bust Down the Door and Eat all the Chickens, and others.

He also edits the Bare Bone anthology series for Raw Dog Screaming Press and does not eat chimpanzees.

Visit him online at myspace.com/kevindonihe

ABOUT THE ILLUSTRATOR

Carlton Mellick III writes bizarro novels and sometimes draws stuff. Visit him online at avantpunk.com

ABOUT THE COVER ARTIST

Lucas Aguirre is a painter from Argentina. Visit his online galleries at www.lucasaguirre.com

Bizarro books

CATALOGUE – SPRING 2006

Bizarro Books publishes under the following imprints:

www.rawdogscreamingpress.com

www.eraserheadpress.com

www.afterbirthbooks.com

www.swallowdownpress.com

For all your Bizarro needs visit:

www.bizarrogenre.org

BB-0X1   "The Bizarro Starter Kit"
An introduction to the Bizarro genre

There's a new genre rising out of the underground. Its name: BIZARRO. For years, readers have been asking for a category of fiction dedicated to the weird, crazy, cult side of storytelling that has become a staple in the film industry (with directors such as David Lynch, Takashi Miike, Tim Burton, and Lloyd Kaufman) but has been largely ignored in the literary world, until now.

THE BIZARRO STARTER KIT features short novels and story collections by ten of the leading authors in the genre: D. Harlan Wilson, Carlton Mellick III, Jeremy Robert Johnson, Kevin L Donihe, Gina Ranalli, Andre Duza, Vincent W. Sakowski, Steve Beard, John Edward Lawson, and Bruce Taylor. Get the perfect sampling of Bizarro for only five dollars plus shipping.

236 pages $5

  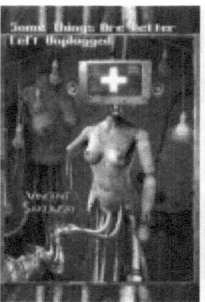 

BB-001"The Kafka Effekt" D. Harlan Wilson - A collection of forty-four irreal short stories loosely written in the vein of Franz Kafka, with more than a pinch of William S. Burroughs sprinkled on top. **211 pages $14**

BB-002 "Satan Burger" Carlton Mellick III - The cult novel that put Carlton Mellick III on the map ... Six punks get jobs at a fast food restaurant owned by the devil in a city violently overpopulated by surreal alien cultures. **236 pages $14**

BB-003 "Some Things Are Better Left Unplugged" Vincent Sakwoski - Join The Man and his Nemesis, the obese tabby, for a nightmare roller coaster ride into this postmodern fantasy. **152 pages $10**

BB-004 "Shall We Gather At the Garden?" Kevin L Donihe - Donihe's Debut novel. Midgets take over the world, The Church of Lionel Richie vs. The Church of the Byrds, plant porn and more! **244 pages $14**

   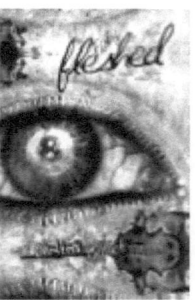

BB-005 "Razor Wire Pubic Hair" Carlton Mellick III - A genderless humandildo is purchased by a razor dominatrix and brought into her nightmarish world of bizarre sex and mutilation. **176 pages $11**

BB-006 "Stranger on the Loose" D. Harlan Wilson - The fiction of Wilson's 2nd collection is planted in the soil of normalcy, but what grows out of that soil is a dark, witty, otherworldly jungle... **228 pages $14**

BB-007 "The Baby Jesus Butt Plug" Carlton Mellick III - Using clones of the Baby Jesus for anal sex will be the hip sex fetish of the future. **92 pages $10**

BB-008 "Fishyfleshed" Carlton Mellick III - The world of the past is an illogical flatland lacking in dimension and color, a sick-scape of crispy squid people wandering the desert for no apparent reason. **260 pages $14**

 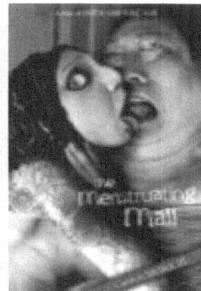  

BB-009 **"Dead Bitch Army"** Andre Duza - Step into a world filled with racist teenagers, cannibals, 100 warped Uncle Sams, automobiles with razor-sharp teeth, living graffiti, and a pissed-off zombie bitch out for revenge.   344 pages $16

BB-010 **"The Menstruating Mall"** Carlton Mellick III   *"The Breakfast Club* meets *Chopping Mall* as directed by David Lynch."* - Brian Keene   212 pages $12

BB-011 **"Angel Dust Apocalypse"** Jeremy Robert Johnson - Meth-heads, manmade monsters, and murderous Neo-Nazis. "Seriously amazing short stories..." - Chuck Palahniuk, author of *Fight Club*   184 pages $11

BB-012 **"Ocean of Lard"**   Kevin L Donihe / Carlton Mellick III - A parody of those old Choose Your Own Adventure kid's books about some very odd pirates sailing on a sea made of animal fat. 176 pages $12

   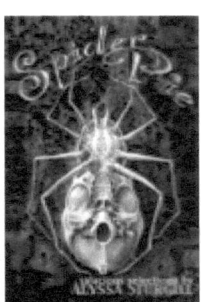

BB-013 **"Last Burn in Hell"** John Edward Lawson - From his lurid angst-affair with a lesbian music diva to his ascendance as unlikely pop icon the one constant for Kenrick Brimley, official state prison gigolo, is he's got no clue what he's doing. 172 pages $14

BB-014 **"Tangerinephant"** Kevin Dole 2 - TV-obsessed aliens have abducted Michael Tangerinephant in this bizarro combination of science fiction, satire, and surrealism. 164 pages $11

BB-015 **"Foop!"**   Chris Genoa - Strange happenings are going on at Dactyl, Inc, the world's first and only time travel tourism company.
"A surreal pie in the face!" - Christopher Moore   300 pages $14

BB-016 **"Spider Pie"** Alyssa Sturgill - A one-way trip down a rabbit hole inhabited by sexual deviants and friendly monsters, fairytale beginnings and hideous endings. 104 pages $11

BB-017 "The Unauthorized Woman" Efrem Emerson - Enter the world of the inner freak, a landscape populated by the pre-dead and morticioners, by cockroaches and 300-lb robots. 104 pages $11

BB-018 "Fugue XXIX" Forrest Aguirre - Tales from the fringe of speculative literary fiction where innovative minds dream up the future's uncharted territories while mining forgotten treasures of the past. 220 pages $16

BB-019 "Pocket Full of Loose Razorblades" John Edward Lawson - A collection of dark bizarro stories. From a giant rectum to a foot-fungus factory to a girl with a biforked tongue. 190 pages $13

BB-020 "Punk Land" Carlton Mellick III - In the punk version of Heaven, the anarchist utopia is threatened by corporate fascism and only Goblin, Mortician's sperm, and a blue-mohawked female assassin named Shark Girl can stop them. 284 pages $15

BB-021 "Pseudo-City" D. Harlan Wilson - Pseudo-City exposes what waits in the bathroom stall, under the manhole cover and in the corporate boardroom, all in a way that can only be described as mind-bogglingly irreal. 220 pages $16

BB-022 "Kafka's Uncle and Other Strange Tales" Bruce Taylor - Anslenot and his giant tarantula (tormentor? fri-end?) wander a desecrated world in this novel and collection of stories from Mr. Magic Realism Himself. 348 pages $17

BB-023 "Sex and Death In Television Town" Carlton Mellick III - In the old west, a gang of hermaphrodite gunslingers take refuge from a demon plague in Telos: a town where its citizens have televisions instead of heads. 184 pages $12

BB-024 "It Came From Below The Belt" Bradley Sands - What can Grover Goldstein do when his severed, sentient penis forces him to return to high school and help it win the presidential election? 204 pages $13

BB-025 "Sick: An Anthology of Illness" John Lawson, editor - These Sick stories are horrendous and hilarious dissections of creative minds on the scalpel's edge. **296 pages $16**

BB-026 "Tempting Disaster" John Lawson, editor - A shocking and alluring anthology from the fringe that examines our culture's obsession with taboos. **260 pages $16**

BB-027 "Siren Promised" Jeremy Robert Johnson - Nominated for the Bram Stoker Award. A potent mix of bad drugs, bad dreams, brutal bad guys, and surreal/incredible art by Alan M. Clark. **190 pages $13**

BB-028 "Chemical Gardens" Gina Ranalli - Ro and punk band *Green is the Enemy* find Kreepkins, a surfer-dude warlock, a vengeful demon, and a Metal Priestess in their way as they try to escape an underground nightmare. **188 pages $13**

BB-029 "Jesus Freaks" Andre Duza For God so loved the world that he gave his only two begotten sons... and a few million zombies. **400 pages $16**

BB-030 "Grape City" Kevin L. Donihe - More Donihe-style comedic bizarro about a demon named Charles who is forced to work a minimum wage job on Earth after Hell goes out of business. **108 pages $10**

BB-031 "Sea of the Patchwork Cats" Carlton Mellick III - A quiet dreamlike tale set in the ashes of the human race. For Mellick enthusiasts who also adore *The Twilight Zone*. **112 pages $10**

BB-032 "Extinction Journals" Jeremy Robert Johnson 104 pages - An uncanny voyage across a newly nuclear America where one man must confront the problems associated with loneliness, insane dieties, radiation, love, and an ever-evolving cockroach suit with a mind of its own. **104 pages $10**

BB-033 "Meat Puppet Cabaret" Steve Beard At last! The secret connection between Jack the Ripper and Princess Diana's death revealed!   240 pages $16 / $30

BB-034 "The Greatest Fucking Moment in Sports" Kevin L. Donihe - In the tradition of the surreal anti-sitcom *Get A Life* comes a tale of triumph and agape love from the master of comedic bizarro.   108 pages $10

BB-035 "The Troublesome Amputee" John Edward Lawson - Disturbing verse from a man who truly believes nothing is sacred and intends to prove it. 104 pages $9

BB-036 "Deity" Vic Mudd God (who doesn't like to be called "God") comes down to a typical, suburban, Ohio family for a little vacation—but it doesn't turn out to be as relaxing as He had hoped it would be...   168 pages $12

BB-037 "The Haunted Vagina" Carlton Mellick III - It's difficult to love a woman whose vagina is a gateway to the world of the dead. 132 pages $10

BB-038 "Tales from the Vinegar Wasteland" Ray Fracalossy - Witness: a man is slowly losing his face, a neighbor who periodically screams out for no apparent reason, and a house with a room that doesn't actually exist.   240 pages $14

BB-039 "Suicide Girls in the Afterlife" Gina Ranalli - After Pogue commits suicide, she unexpectedly finds herself an unwilling "guest" at a hotel in the Afterlife, where she meets a group of bizarre characters, including a goth Satan, a hippie Jesus, and an alien-human hybrid.   100 pages $9

BB-040 "And Your Point Is?" Steve Aylett - In this follow-up to LINT multiple authors provide critical commentary and essays about Jeff Lint's mind-bending literature. 104 pages $11

BB-041 "Not Quite One of the Boys" Vincent Sakowski -While drug-dealer Maxi drinks with Dante in purgatory, God and Satan play a little tri-level chess and do a little bargaining over his business partner, Vinnie, who is still left on earth.   220 pages $14

COMING SOON:

"Misadventures in a Thumbnail Universe" by Vincent Sakowski

"House of Houses" by Kevin Donihe

"War Slut" by Carlton Mellick III

ORDER FORM

TITLES	QTY	PRICE	TOTAL
Shipping costs (see below)			
TOTAL			

Please make checks and moneyorders payable to ROSE O'KEEFE / BIZARRO BOOKS in U.S. funds only. Please don't send bad checks! Allow 2-6 weeks for delivery. International orders may take longer. If you'd like to pay online via PAYPAL.COM, send payments to publisher@eraserheadpress.com.

SHIPPING: US ORDERS - $2 for the first book, $1 for each additional book. For priority shipping, add an additional $4. INT'L ORDERS - $5 for the first book, $3 for each additional book. Add an additional $5 per book for global priority shipping.

Send payment to:

  BIZARRO BOOKS
    C/O Rose O'Keefe
    205 NE Bryant
    Portland, OR 97211

Name	
Address	
City	State Zip
Country	
Email	Phone